What is phonics?

Phonics helps children learn to read and write by teaching them the letter sounds (known as phonemes), rather than the letter names, e.g. the sound that 'c' makes rather than its alphabetic name. They then learn how to blend the sounds: the process of saying the sounds in a word or 'sounding out' and then blending them together to make the word, for example c – a – t = cat. Once the phonemes and the skill of blending are learnt, children can tackle reading any phonetically decodable word they come across, even ones they don't know, with confidence and success.

However, there are of course many words in the English language that aren't phonetically decodable, e.g. if a child gets stuck on 'the' it doesn't help if they sound it out and blend it. We call these 'tricky words' and they are just taught as words that are so 'tricky' that children have to learn to recognise them by sight.

How do phonic readers work?

Phonic reading books are written especially for children who are beginning to learn phonics at nursery or school, and support any programme being used by providing plenty of practice as children develop the skills of decoding and blending. By targeting specific phonemes and tricky words, increasing in difficulty, they ensure systematic progression with reading.

Because phonic readers are primarily decodable – aside from the target tricky words which need to be learnt, children should be able to read the books with real assurance and accomplishment.

Big Cat phonic readers:
Zog and Zebra

In Big Cat phonic readers the specific phonemes and tricky words being focussed on are highlighted here in these notes, so that you can be clear about what your child's learning and what they need to practise.

While reading at home together, there are all sorts of fun additional games you can play to help your child practise those phonemes and tricky words, which can be a nice way to familiarise yourselves with them before reading, or remind you of them after you've finished. In *Zog and Zebra*, for example:

- the focus phonemes are z (Zog), qu (quiver), ay (play), ea (eat), a-e (shake), i-e (hide). Why not write them down and encourage your child to practise saying the sounds as you point to them in a random order. This is called 'Speed Sounds' and as you get faster and faster with your pointing, it encourages your child to say them as quickly as possible. You can try reversing the roles, so that you have a practice too!

- the tricky words are 'saw', 'what', 'have', 'some', 'where', 'so', 'who', 'you', 'was' and 'said'. You can play 'Hide and Seek' by asking your child to close their eyes and count to 10, while you write each word on a piece of paper, hiding them somewhere in the room you're in or the garden for your child to find. As they find each one, they should try reading and spelling the word out.

Reading together

- Why not start by looking at the front cover of *Zog and Zebra* and talking about what you can see.

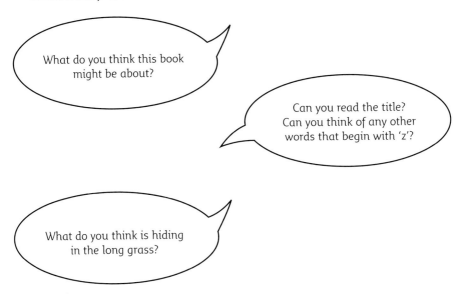

What do you think this book might be about?

Can you read the title? Can you think of any other words that begin with 'z'?

What do you think is hiding in the long grass?

- Enjoy reading *Zog and Zebra* together, noticing the focus phonemes (z, qu, ay, ea, a-e, i-e) and tricky words (saw, what, have, some, where, so, who, you, was, said). It's useful to point to each word as your child reads, and encouraging to give them lots of praise as they go.

- If your child gets stuck on a word, and it's phonetically decodable, encourage them to sound it out. You can practise blending by saying the sounds aloud a few times, getting quicker and quicker. If they still can't read it, tell them the word and move on.

Talking about the book

- Use the story map on pp18–19 to retell the story together, and talk about how Zog and Zebra feel at different points of the story.

- Practise the focus phonemes from *Zog and Zebra* by asking your child to find specific words with, for example, the 'ea' phoneme, or sounding out some of the key words, for example, 'play'.

Zog and Zebra

Written by Mal Peet and
Elspeth Graham
Illustrated by Sarah Horne

Collins

Zog was zooming around in
his flying ship.
He had found a lovely planet.
"Just where I can have
my lunch," said Zog.

Zog landed on the ground and looked around.

He was hungry so he got his picnic basket.
"I will have lunch and then I will look around," said Zog.

Zog saw Zebra.
"I am Zog," said Zog.
"My name is Zebra,"
said Zebra.
"I like your stripes," said Zog.
"Have some of my picnic."

After lunch Zog and Zebra
went to play.
"Shall we play hide and seek?"
asked Zebra.
"You hide and I will count
to ten," said Zog.

Zebra hid in the trees.
Zog looked for Zebra.
His stripes made him hard
to see.

10

Next Zog hid. He was very
quiet and very still.
What was that?

Zog saw the long grass
shake and quiver.
Something was hidden in it.

It was a big cat! The big cat was not playing. He was creeping up on Zebra. The big cat wanted to eat Zebra.

"Look out!" shouted Zog as he ran to help Zebra.

Zog jumped on Zebra and
they ran away. Zebra was safe!
But it was getting late
and Zog had to leave.

Zog and Zebra felt sad.
"I will miss you, Zebra,"
said Zog.
"Who will I play with?"
said Zebra.
Zog and Zebra had a big hug.

As Zog took off he felt a tear slip down his cheek. Then he had a plan ...

"I will go back," said Zog and he zoomed back to Zebra.

"Come with me," said Zog.
It was a squeeze getting Zebra
into the flying ship. Zog was
huffing and puffing but soon
Zebra was in.

Zebra and Zog were
very happy.
"This is fun!" they shouted.
They waved to the big cat
and zoomed off to look for
new planets.

A story map

Getting creative

- Have some fun with your child by asking them to paint or draw the focus phonemes from *Zog and Zebra* in bright colours.

- Challenge them to guess which tricky word you're thinking of as you give them clues, for example, 'I begin with w and I have a tricky sound in the middle.'

- If your child's enjoyed reading about Zog and Zebra, you could ask them what they think Zog and Zebra might do next.

- They could start by drawing a picture of what they think they'll do next, and then start writing their own Zog and Zebra adventure.

Other books at Level 2:

Fiction	Non-fiction
A Day Out — Petr Horáček	The Sun and the Moon — Paul Shipton
The Singing Beetle — Linda Strachan, Oliver Hurst	The Rainforest at Night — Nic Bishop
Zog and Zebra — Mal Peet and Elspeth Graham, Sarah Horne	Gorillas — Teresa Heapy

Collins Big Cat
Reading Lions

Published by Collins
An imprint of HarperCollins*Publishers*
1 London Bridge Street
London
SE1 9GF

© HarperCollins*Publishers* Limited 2013
This edition was published in 2015.

Authors: Mal Peet and Elspeth Graham

British Library Cataloguing in Publication Data
A catalogue record for this publication is available from the British Library.

Illustrator: Sarah Horne
Designer: Niki Merrett
Parent notes authors: Sue Reed and Liz Webster

Printed and bound by RR Donnelley APS

www.collins.co.uk/parents